This
Treasure Cove Story
belongs to

SPONGE IN SPACE!

A CENTUM BOOK 978-1-912396-22-1
Published in Great Britain by Centum Books Ltd.
This edition published 2018. 1 3 5 7 9 10 8 6 4 2

Centum Books Ltd, 20 Devon Square, Newton Abbot,
Devon, TQ12 2HR, UK.

www.centumbooksltd.co.uk | books@centumbooksltd.co.uk
CENTUM BOOKS Limited Reg.No. 07641486.

A CIP catalogue record for this book is available
from the British Library.

Printed in China.

centum

nickelodeon

A Treasure Cove Story

SPONGEBOB SQUAREPANTS

Sponge in Space!

Adapted by Melissa Wygand • Illustrated by Heather Martinez

Based on the screenplay *'Sandy's Rocket'* by Sherm Cohen,
Aaron Springer and Peter Burns

Created by

Stephen Hillenburg

One day, SpongeBob went to visit his
friend Sandy. When SpongeBob got to the
Treedome, he couldn't believe his eyes.
Sandy had a rocket!

'I'm going to the moon tomorrow,'
Sandy said.

SpongeBob asked if he could go, too.
'I want to see aliens — and I don't take
up much room.'

'Sure, you can come on the space trip
with me, SpongeBob,' Sandy replied. 'But
there are no aliens on the moon.'

That night, SpongeBob was too excited to sleep. He couldn't stop thinking about his trip to outer space the next day.

SpongeBob would steer the speeding rocket
up into space, zooming past stars and comets.

And he would boldly explore strange planets.

SpongeBob didn't believe what Sandy
had said about aliens. He knew he would
meet bizarre beings on the moon.
   'I'm not scared of aliens,' SpongeBob
told himself. 'There are strange creatures
everywhere.'

Suddenly, Patrick popped through
SpongeBob's window.

'I heard about your trip, SpongeBob,'
said Patrick. 'We have to make Sandy's
rocket alien-proof.'

SpongeBob thought that was an
excellent idea.

SpongeBob gave Patrick a tour of the rocket. Patrick was amazed.

'I wonder which button makes the rocket go,' Patrick said.

'This one,' replied SpongeBob.

The rocket **RUMBLED**. Flames shot
from its engine. The rocket began to rise
higher and higher into the sky.

The rocket went faster and faster as it flew into space. Suddenly, SpongeBob and Patrick were weightless.

'Wow!' exclaimed SpongeBob. 'What a weird feeling! It's like we're swimming, but it's floatier!'

The rocket headed for the moon, missed it, and sped back to Earth. SpongeBob and Patrick landed with a **THUD**.

'Who turned the heavy back on?' groaned Patrick.

But SpongeBob and Patrick didn't realize that
the rocket had landed back in Bikini Bottom.
They thought they were on the moon!

'Wow, this looks like home,' Patrick said.

'No. It's a trick,' whispered SpongeBob. 'We
must explore! But we have to be very careful.'

'We found an alien!' exclaimed
SpongeBob. 'Look at its tentacles... its
giant fleshy head... its huge nose! It's
horrible! We have to capture it and bring
it back to Earth.'

SpongeBob threw a net
over the alien.
'I'll prove to Sandy that
aliens do exist,' he said.

Just then, Sandy appeared. 'What are you doing, SpongeBob?' she asked.

SpongeBob gulped. 'That alien is pretending to be Sandy! It even knows my name!'

'The aliens are reading our thoughts and trying to control our minds!' he warned Patrick. 'They're tricky — but we have nets!'

SpongeBob and Patrick captured Sandy.

They got Mr Krabs.

And they netted Mrs Puff and Gary.
Soon they had caught everyone in Bikini Bottom.

When they were finished, Patrick realized something. 'If the aliens can trick us,' he said to SpongeBob, 'how do I know you're really you and I'm really me?'

SpongeBob and Patrick grabbed their nets and stared at each other suspiciously.

Patrick struck first... and caught himself!
SpongeBob couldn't wait to show Sandy all
the aliens he'd captured!

'Next stop: Bikini Bottom!' exclaimed SpongeBob.

The rocket shot into space again, but
this time it ran out of fuel. It sputtered
and wheezed... and landed on the moon!

'SpongeBob, we *aliens* want to have a word with you,' said Sandy. 'Does anyone know how to fix rockets?' asked SpongeBob.

Treasure Cove Stories

1 Three Little Pigs
2 Snow White
& The Seven Dwarfs
3 The Fox and the Hound
- Hide and Seek
4 Dumbo
5 Cinderella
6 Cinderella's Friends
7 Alice In Wonderland
8 Mad Hatter's Tea Party
from Alice In Wonderland
9 Mickey Mouse and
his Spaceship
10 Peter Pan
11 Pinocchio
12 Mickey Mouse Flies
the Christmas Mail
13 Sleeping Beauty
and the Good Fairies
14 The Lucky Puppy
15 Chicken Little
16 Mother Goose
17 Coco
18 Winnie-the-Pooh and Tigger
19 The Sword in the Stone
20 Mary Poppins
21 The Jungle Book
22 Aristocats
23 Lady and the Tramp
24 Bambi
25 Bambi - Friends
of the Forest
26 Pete's Dragon
27 Beauty & The Beast
- The Teapot's Tale
28 Monsters, Inc.
- M is for Monster
29 Finding Nemo
30 The Incredibles
31 The Incredibles
- Jack-Jack Attack
32 Ratatouille
- Your Friend the Rat
33 Wall-E
34 Up
35 Princess and the Frog

36 Toy Story - The Pet Problem
37 Dora the Explorer - Dora and
the Unicorn King
38 Dora the Explorer
- Grandma's House
39 Spider-Man
- Night of the Vulture!
40 Wreck-it Ralph
41 Brave
42 The Invincible Iron Man
- Eye of the Dragon
43 SpongeBob SquarePants
- Sponge in Space!
44 SpongeBob SquarePants
- Where the Pirates Arrrgh!
45 Toy Story - A Roaring
Adventure
46 Cars - Deputy Mater
Saves the Day!
47 Spider-Man
- Trapped By The Green Goblin
48 Big Hero 6
49 Spider-Man - High Voltage!
50 Frozen
51 Cinderella Is My Babysitter
52 Beauty & The Beast
- I Am The Beast
53 Blaze and the Monster
Machines - Mighty Monster
Machines
54 Blaze and the Monster
Machines - Dino Parade!
55 Teenage Mutant Ninja Turtles
- Follow The Ninja!
56 I Am A Princess
57 Paw Patrol
- The Big Book of Paw Patrol
58 Paw Patrol
- Adventures with Grandpa
59 Merida Is My Babysitter
60 Trolls
61 Trolls Holiday Special
62 The Secret Life of Pets
63 Zootropolis
64 Ariel Is My Babysitter
65 Inside Out

66 Belle Is My Babysitter
67 The Lion Guard
- Eye In The Sky
68 Moana
69 Finding Dory
70 Guardians of the Galaxy
71 Captain America
- High-Stakes Heist!
72 Ant-Man
73 The Mighty Avengers
74 The Mighty Avengers
- Lights Out!
75 The Incredible Hulk
76 Shimmer & Shine
- Wish upon a Sleepover
77 Shimmer & Shine
- Backyard Ballet
78 Paw Patrol - All-Star Pups!
79 Teenage Mutant Ninja Turtles
- Really Spaced Out!
80 Cars 2 - Travel Buddies
81 Madagascar
82 Jasmine Is My Babysitter
83 How To Train Your Dragon
84 Shrek
85 Puss In Boots
86 Kung Fu Panda
87 Beauty & The Beast
- I Am Belle
88 The Lion Guard
- The Imaginary Okapi
89 Thor - Thunder Strike
90 Guardians of the Galaxy
-Rocket to the Rescue
91 Nella The Princess Knight
- Nella and the Dragon
92 Shimmer & Shine
- Treasure Twins!
93 Olaf's Frozen Adventure
94 Black Panther
95 Branch's Bunker Birthday
96 Shimmer & Shine
- Pet Talent Show

Book list may be subject to change.

An ongoing series to collect and enjoy!